The Moose and the Goose at Nottingham Square

by Carol Ann Stevenson

AuthorHouse™
1663 Liberty Drive
Bloomington, IN 47403
www.authorhouse.com
Phone: 833-262-8899

Because of the dynamic nature of the Internet, any web addresses or links contained in this book may have changed
since publication and may no longer be valid. The views expressed in this work are solely those of the author and do not
necessarily reflect the views of the publisher, and the publisher hereby disclaims any responsibility for them.

This book is printed on acid-free paper.

Interior Image Credit: Tambrey Jolenia Daggett

ISBN: 978-1-6655-0645-8 (sc)
ISBN: 978-1-6655-0647-2 (hc)
ISBN: 978-1-6655-0646-5 (e)

Library of Congress Control Number: 2020921696

Print information available on the last page.

Published by AuthorHouse 11/06/2020

authorHOUSE®

To My Loving Children:
Dean, Lee & Dana
And My Grand & Great
Grandchildren!
Love Mom

About the Illustrator:
Tambrey Jolenia Of Newmarket, NH with her great talent for painting and sculpting received an award from Newmarket High, Scholarship to Cranbrook Art Academy in the state of Michigan. She also received a college grant at UNH for Fine Arta.

In Nottingham Town
There was a green square
The houses around it
See white and quite bare.

IT was sleepy and
Quite most of the year
But... something happened
That caused immense fear!

A goose and a moose
Stepped off the bus
And with their arrival
Created a fuss!

The town folk did not
Want to fancy this pair
They were so different
From anyone there.

The story begins
At the square so neat
Where people would go
Just to talk and meet.

Because on that square
There was a grey goose
His name was Maury
And he loved the brown moose.

Her name was Minni
They were quite a pair
The town had not seen
Their likes on the square.

He was dark grey
And she chestnut brown
Together, unusual
In Nottingham Town.

The people would come
From far off to stare
At the goose and the moose
Strutting around the square.

Maury had a top hat
And carried a cane
Minnie wore a hat
You would not see again.

It had flowers and
Birds and bees galore
With out even a tag
To tell from what store.

Where did the moose find
A hat such as that?
With flowers and bees
And a dove so fat.

The folks round the square
Would ask one another
Oh, now, what is that?
They've added an umbrella!

The umbrella was red
With big stripes of white
And the tassels of gold
It was quite a sight.

The goose and the moose
The hat and the cane
The red and white umbrella
Soon brought the great fame!

They wrote in the paper
"The Nottingham Times"
Of the goose and the moose
That were dressed to the nines.

The famous and colorful
With umbrella and hats
They soon grew tired of
Being followed by cats.

So, they walked in the square
For one final round
And furled their umbrella
And bowed to the crowed.

Of Nottingham Square they
They had seen enough
It was now time to leave
So they boarded the bus.

As the bus drove from town
The crowd gave a great cheer!
And Minni and Maury
They waved from the rear.

The window was open
And out their hats flew
The last they were seen
The umbrella went too.

A pretty blue spruce
Was standing right there
The hats and umbrella
Got caught in its hair.

The colors were awesome
The tree looked so fair
The town folk decided
To leave them right there.

The goose and the moose
Themselves unbeknownst
Had left an impression
On the town folk the most.

Their story of love that
Comes but once in awhile
The town folk and cats
Could just stand there and smile.

For they had just witnessed
A love so divine
Everyone knew it
Would last for all time.

Was a goose and a moose
But mattered not a hair
Cause love was the answer
And they were a pair.

Nottingham changed for
The better that day
The town folk all wished
That they come there to stay.

A lesson was learned
(Alas and Alack!)
Do not judge others
By their colors or hats!

Lightning Source UK Ltd.
Milton Keynes UK
UKHW051016301120
374352UK00006B/83